THE LAST HURRAH

ASHOK JAHAGIRDAR

Made with ♥ on the Notion Press Platform
www.notionpress.com

Contents

CHAPTER ONE

Echoes of Yesterday

Jack Mcenroe wasn't quite sure what had drawn him back to Glenfield after all these years. Maybe it was nostalgia, a tug at the heart that made the past feel like a place worth revisiting. Or maybe it was the letter he'd received just a month ago, crumpled and stuffed into his mailbox, a hastily scrawled note from his old friend, Dan McKinney - Come back. This town could use someone who still believes in the truth.

Jack hadn't thought of himself as someone who still "believed" in anything. The years in the newspaper business had worn him thin, chewed him up, and spat him out, leaving only a shell of the wide-eyed kid who'd left Glenfield decades ago with big dreams and a reporter's notebook. Now he was back, a stranger in his own hometown, and he felt the weight of it in every slow step that he took on Main Street.

The town hadn't changed much, he thought as he strolled past the familiar storefronts. The hardware store still had that hand-painted sign with faded red letters, and Joe,s Diner sat as stoic as ever, with its big bay window and cracked green vinyl booths. The only thing different was Jack himself. He was older now, his hair speckled with grey, his face lined with the stories he'd written—and maybe even more with the ones he'd chosen not to.

As he walked, Jack caught sight of the courthouse at the end of the block, its tall columns standing like sentinels. A wave of memories washed over him—days spent chasing stories here, long afternoons listening to Dan preach about justice and change from the courthouse steps, back when they'd both been young and hungry for something more.

Dan. It was always about Dan, wasn't it?

Jack hadn't spoken to his old friend in over a decade, and he could still feel the sting of their last conversation. It had been an argument—loud, bitter, full of accusations. Dan had accused Jack of betraying him, of putting his career over their friendship, and Jack had shot back that Dan wasn't half the hero he pretended to be. They'd left it there, words sharp and jagged, wounds left open to fester.

Yet here he was, back in Glenfield, carrying a heavy suitcase and even heavier memories.

Jack stopped in front of the town's memorial fountain, watching the water ripple in the early autumn breeze. He remembered when Dan had organized its dedication years ago, insisting that every name of the town's fallen soldiers be engraved in marble. Dan had spoken that day about honour and sacrifice, about what it meant to give everything for something greater than yourself. Jack had watched from the sidelines, feeling a strange mixture of pride and unease, as though he already knew that Dan's words would one day come back to haunt him.

"You're back."

The voice startled Jack out of his thoughts. He turned to see Meg Bryant , the editor of the Glenfield Gazette, standing a few feet away, arms crossed, her eyes sharp beneath a shock of silver hair. She was older now, too, but still fierce, still the woman who'd been a mentor to him when he was fresh out of college and barely knew how to hold a pen.

"Meg," he said, managing a smile. "Didn't expect you to be here."

She shrugged. "I could say the same to you." Her eyes softened, just a touch. "Dan said you'd come."

Jack glanced away, feeling a pang of something he couldn't quite name. Regret? Shame? He'd buried those feelings deep a long time ago. "He called me out of the blue. Said he needed someone to 'document the truth.' He always did have a way with words."

"Dan's running for mayor," Meg said, as if that explained everything. "He thinks he can fix this town, save it from itself. Sounds like a tall order, doesn't it?"

Jack laughed, but it was a hollow sound. "Dan always did like playing the hero."

Meg looked at him with something that might have been pity. "People can change, Jack. Maybe he really is trying to do some good."

Jack wasn't so sure. Dan had always been good at wearing masks, slipping into whatever role suited him best. In their youth, it had been the charming activist, the crusader with fire in his eyes and a plan to change the world. But as they grew older, Jack had seen a different side—a side that was willing to compromise, to make deals in back rooms, to trade loyalty for ambition. It was that side that had driven a wedge between them, made Jack question everything he'd ever known about his best friend.

"Maybe," he murmured, watching the fountain. "Or maybe he just wants one last shot at redemption."

Meg tilted her head, studying him. "And what about you, Jack? What are you looking for?"

He didn't answer, because he didn't know. All he knew was that he felt like a ghost in this town, haunted by memories that had lost their shape, by a friendship that had turned to dust in his hands. He was here because Dan had asked, because some part of him needed to see this story through, to find closure—if that was even possible.

"Guess I'll find out," he said finally, giving Meg a tight smile. "Got any good leads for an old reporter?"

She chuckled, gesturing toward the courthouse. "Start with Dan. He's holding a town hall tomorrow night, kicking off his campaign. If you're looking for a story, I'd bet my typewriter that you'll find it there."

Jack watched her walk away, her silhouette fading into the golden afternoon light. He felt a strange sense of anticipation, a whisper of something he hadn't felt in years.

He wasn't sure if he was here to save Dan or to bury him. But one thing was certain—this was his last story, and he would tell it the way it deserved to be told.

Tomorrow, he'd go to the town hall. And maybe, just maybe, he'd find the answers he'd been running from all these years.

CHAPTER TWO

A Friendship Torn

The next evening, Jack stood outside the old high school auditorium, a place he hadn't set foot in since graduation. Memories washed over him—the pep rallies, the graduation ceremony, the countless speeches Dan had given even back then, when he was just a kid with big ideas and an infectious charisma. Back then, everyone thought he'd change the world, and Jack had been his most loyal believer.

Inside, the auditorium buzzed with chatter as townsfolk filled the seats, bundled in flannel jackets and worn coats. Some things never changed. Glenfield wasn't the kind of place that gave in to fashion trends or new ideas without a good fight. It was a town that clung to its traditions, and Dan Winters was banking on that loyalty.

Jack slipped into a seat in the back, unnoticed, his old notebook resting on his lap. He felt a strange nervousness—an unease he hadn't felt since his early days in journalism. He wasn't just here to cover a story; he was here to confront the man who'd once been his best friend, to make sense of the tangled history they shared.

The lights dimmed, and the room fell quiet as Dan stepped onto the stage. He looked older, though he still had that easy charm, that natural confidence that made people want to believe in him. His hair was flecked with grey, his face lined with years of political battles and hard decisions. But he held himself tall, his gaze steady, as if he had already won.

Jack watched as Dan took a moment to scan the crowd, his eyes briefly flickering over the audience before landing on him. For a split second, their eyes met, and Jack felt a flash of something he couldn't quite name. Surprise? Recognition? Or maybe just a lingering hurt that neither of them had ever fully dealt with.

"Thank you all for coming," Dan began, his voice calm and steady, filling the room with a practiced warmth. "I've lived in this town my entire life. Glenfield isn't just a place to me; it's home. It's where I grew up, where I learned the values of hard work, honesty, and community."

The crowd murmured approvingly, and Jack could see the glimmers of admiration in their faces. Dan had always had a way with words, a way of making people feel like he was speaking directly to them. But Jack knew better than to be charmed. He knew Dan's story too well.

"I know Glenfield has had its troubles," Dan continued. "I know we've been through our share of hardships—lost jobs, empty storefronts, families struggling to make ends meet. But I believe in this town. I believe that together, we can turn things around."

Applause rippled through the room, and Jack felt a pang of bitterness. This was the Dan he remembered—the Dan who could rally a room, who could inspire hope with nothing more than a few carefully chosen words. But he'd seen the other side of that coin too—the deals Dan had made, the compromises he'd accepted, the small betrayals that had chipped away at the man Jack had once admired.

As Dan spoke, painting a vision of a brighter future, Jack's mind drifted back to the early days of their friendship. They'd been inseparable then, two young men who wanted to change the world. Jack had been the idealist, eager to expose injustices, to shine a light on the darker corners of society. Dan had been the pragmatist, the one who believed that change required strategy, negotiation, and, sometimes, sacrifice.

But somewhere along the line, Dan's sacrifices had stopped being about others and had become about his own ambitions. Jack could still remember the first time he'd seen it—a story he'd written, an expose on a corrupt local contractor who'd been skimming money from public projects. Jack had been proud of the article, certain it would bring about change. But Dan had pulled him aside, warning him to be careful, to think about the consequences.

"Not every truth needs to be told, Jack," Dan had said, his voice a quiet plea. "Sometimes, the bigger picture matters more."

At the time, Jack hadn't understood. He'd thought Dan was just being cautious, maybe even naïve. But over the years, he'd come to realize that Dan had been willing to make compromises he couldn't stomach. Jack had wanted to save the world, while Dan had learned how to play the game. And it was that game that had eventually torn them apart.

Dan's voice pulled him back to the present. "I won't promise miracles," he was saying, his tone humble, grounded. "But I can promise this: I'll fight for you. I'll fight for this town, for the people who've given me everything. Together, we can make Glenfield a place we're proud to call home."

The applause was louder this time, filled with a genuine fervour that seemed to fill every corner of the room. Jack watched Dan step down from the stage, shaking hands, clapping backs, exchanging words of gratitude with the people who had come to support him.

As the crowd thinned, Jack felt the weight of the years between them, the years that had shaped them into men neither one fully recognized. He waited until the room was nearly empty, watching as Dan turned and, at last, approached him.

"Jack," Dan said, his voice softer now, edged with something that might have been regret. "Didn't think you'd actually come."

"Didn't think I'd get the invitation," Jack replied, his tone cool, guarded.

Dan chuckled, but there was no humour in it. "I figured you'd want one last story before you hung up the pen. And who better to write it than the man who's been my biggest critic?"

Jack shook his head. "I'm not here to tear you down, Dan. I'm not here to get o tear you down. I'm here to simply get the truth."

Dan's expression darkened, his gaze shifting to the floor. "Truth," he murmured, almost as if it were a foreign word. "I don't know if there's much left of that anymore, Jack. Not after all this time."

"Maybe that's why I'm here," Jack replied. "Maybe I want to find out if there's anything left of the man I used to know."

Dan looked up, and for a moment, Jack saw a flicker of vulnerability, a crack in the carefully constructed facade. "I'm still that man, Jack. I've just... learned a few hard lessons along the way."

Jack's gaze was steady, unyielding. "Hard lessons, or hard compromises?"

Dan's jaw clenched, but he didn't answer. Instead, he placed a hand on Jack's shoulder, his grip firm, almost desperate. "Just... give me a chance to prove myself. Give me one last chance."

Jack wanted to believe him. He wanted to believe that his old friend was still in there somewhere, that there was still something worth saving. But years of disappointment, of watching Dan lose pieces of himself to ambition, had left him wary, guarded.

"Fine," he said finally, pulling his shoulder free. "I'll give you a chance, Dan. But I'm not here to help you. I'm here to write the truth, whatever that turns out to be."

Dan's face tightened, his expression unreadable. "Fair enough," he replied, his voice barely above a whisper. "I guess that's all I can ask for."

As he walked away, Jack felt a hollow ache in his chest—a sadness for the friend he'd lost, and a fear that he might never find him again. He had come back to Glenfield hoping to close a chapter of his life, but he was beginning to realize that some stories didn't have simple endings. Some stories were like wounds that refused to heal, memories that lingered, haunting the quiet spaces of the heart.

For Jack, this was the beginning of his last story. But he couldn't shake the feeling that it might also be the beginning of a reckoning—one that would force him to confront not just Dan's choices, but his own.

CHAPTER THREE

Old Ghosts and New Scandals

The next morning, Jack sat at the corner booth in Joe's Diner, his old haunt from back when he and Dan were kids. It was a chilly morning, and steam rose from his coffee as he sipped, eyes scanning the Glenfield Gazette headline: "A New Beginning for Glenfield?"

The article was optimistic, hailing Dan's campaign kickoff as a fresh start. The piece was written with a hopeful tone Jack found hard to relate to, knowing what he did about his old friend. Dan's last-minute bid for mayor was being framed as a selfless attempt to give back to the community, but Jack couldn't shake the feeling that there was more to it—a desperate need to rewrite his legacy before it was too late.

The bell above the diner door chimed, and Jack looked up, surprised to see Tom Blanchard, the town's longtime contractor and local power player. Tom was the kind of man whose wealth and connections kept him protected, even when whispers of shady deals and corner-cutting circulated. He spotted Jack and, with a sly smile, made his way over.

"Well, well," Tom said, sliding into the booth across from Jack. "Look who the cat dragged in."

Jack forced a polite nod. "Tom. Been a while."

"Been too long," Tom said, though his grin suggested otherwise. "You back here to write a piece on our hometown hero?"

Jack's gaze hardened. "I'm here to get the story, Tom. Whatever that turns out to be."

Tom chuckled, his tone growing slick. "Right, right. Dig up all the old dirt, I imagine. Well, you'd better bring a big shovel, because I doubt you'll find much."

Jack leaned forward, his voice low. "Funny, I don't remember you being this interested in local politics. What's your angle here?"

Tom's face barely shifted, but there was a glint of something dangerous in his eyes. "Glenfield's my town too, Jack. I have a vested interest in seeing it run by someone who understands the balance between, let's say, dreams and reality."

Jack understood the subtext. Men like Tom were always on the lookout for people they could influence, people who owed them something. And Dan, despite his charisma, had always been more vulnerable to that influence than he'd let on.

"Dan's playing with fire if he's in bed with you, Tom," Jack said, his tone sharp.

Tom's smile didn't waver. "We're all just trying to keep Glenfield afloat. Isn't that why you came back? To be a part of the solution?"

"I came back for the truth," Jack replied.

Tom stood, brushing imaginary dust from his shirt. "Careful, Jack. Digging up the past can be dangerous work. Not everyone wants to see old wounds reopened." With that, he turned and left, leaving Jack alone with his coffee and a sense of unease that was growing stronger by the minute.

That evening, Jack found himself at the Glenfield Community Center, where Dan was hosting another town hall. The building was packed, filled with familiar faces—neighbours, old classmates, even his former high school teacher, Mrs. Abernathy, still holding court among her fellow retirees.

Dan was at the front of the room, his charm on full display, moving effortlessly from person to person, shaking hands, making promises. Jack watched, feeling both admiration and frustration. Dan was still that same magnetic force he'd been in their youth, but there was a sharpness, a desperation beneath the surface that hadn't been there before.

At one point, Dan spotted Jack in the crowd and made his way over, giving him a cautious smile.

"Didn't expect you to actually come," Dan said, folding his arms.

Jack nodded. "Thought it might be worth seeing how things have changed since I left."

Dan's smile faded slightly. "You don't have to look for trouble, Jack. Sometimes, things are exactly what they seem."

"Are they?" Jack challenged, lowering his voice. "Because from where I'm standing, it looks like you're in deep with Tom Rourke and the people he keeps around. And that doesn't exactly scream 'clean slate.'"

Dan's jaw tightened, his eyes narrowing. "Tom is a businessman. He's invested in Glenfield's future. Nothing wrong with that."

"Unless his 'investment' is just his way of buying influence." Jack held Dan's gaze, searching for a sign that his old friend was still in there. "Tell me you're not letting him pull your strings, Dan."

Dan looked away, a flicker of guilt crossing his face. "I know what I'm doing, Jack. I don't need a lecture from someone who left this town behind years ago."

Jack felt a pang of anger and hurt. "I didn't leave Glenfield, Dan. I left a version of this place that I couldn't believe in anymore. And maybe I thought... maybe I thought you'd be different by now."

Dan's expression softened, but only for a moment. "People change, Jack. And sometimes, we have to make choices we don't like to get things done."

Jack took a deep breath, his frustration bubbling over. "So that's it, then? You're just going to sell your soul to win this election?"

Dan met his gaze, his voice barely a whisper. "It's not that simple. Glenfield needs help, and I'm the only one who can make it happen. If you can't understand that... maybe you don't know me as well as you think."

Jack stared at him, feeling a strange sense of loss. He could see that Dan believed in what he was saying, that he genuinely thought he was doing what was best. But Jack had seen this story before—people justifying compromises, letting little lies slip by, until they became something unrecognizable.

"Maybe I don't," Jack said finally. "But that doesn't mean I won't try to find out."

Dan looked away, a shadow of something unreadable crossing his face. "Do what you have to, Jack. But don't expect me to be the same person I was back then."

As Dan moved back to the crowd, Jack felt a weight settle over him. He had come to Glenfield looking for answers, hoping to find some semblance of the man he'd once trusted. But instead, he was left with even more questions, a tangled mess of loyalties and regrets that seemed to stretch further back than he'd realized.

After the event, Jack decided to follow up on a hunch. He drove to the Glenfield courthouse and, using his press credentials, requested access to recent financial records related to the town's infrastructure projects. As he poured over spreadsheets and receipts under the fluorescent lights of the records office, a pattern began to emerge—a trail of contracts awarded to companies owned by Tom's associates, bids that had seemed strangely generous in their estimates.

Jack's hands tightened around the papers, feeling the familiar pulse of adrenaline that came with the scent of a story. This wasn't just a campaign for Dan; it was a cover-up. The town's budget was being funnelled into private pockets under the guise of "public projects." And Dan, whether he knew it or not, was caught up in it all.

He sat back, a chill settling over him. The story he'd come here to write was bigger than he'd realized, and it was about to pull him—and Dan—deeper than either of them had ever imagined.

For the first time, Jack wondered if he had come back to Glenfield to find the truth, or if he had come back to bury it.

CHAPTER FOUR

The Unravelling

Jack barely slept that night. The courthouse files haunted him, like puzzle pieces whispering of something far darker than just political ambition. He had spent years exposing stories just like this—corrupt officials, shady contracts, the usual rot that festered in the shadows. But it was different this time. This time, the man at the centre of it all was someone he had once called a friend.

As the first light of dawn slipped through his window, Jack gulped down a pot of coffee, grabbed his notebook, and reviewed his notes. He knew he was about to open a Pandora's box, one that could shatter what little was left of his relationship with Dan. But he also knew that he couldn't turn back. Not now.

Later that morning, Jack made his way to Dan's campaign headquarters—a small office crammed into an old building on Main Street. He felt a wave of nostalgia as he walked past the diner, the bookstore, and the hardware store where he'd worked part-time as a teenager. Glenfield had barely changed on the outside, but he knew its core was crumbling. He wondered if Dan saw it too—or if he was too deep to notice.

Inside the office, Jack was greeted by Jenny Jackson, Dan's campaign manager. She was young, sharp-eyed, with a no-nonsense air about her. She didn't look surprised to see Jack.

"Jack Mcenroe," she said, sizing him up. "You're either here to help or to tear this place apart. Which is it?"

Jack raised his hands, trying to look harmless. "I just need to speak with Dan. It's... personal."

Jenny's gaze softened slightly, but her guard didn't drop. "I don't know if he has time for personal, Jack. This campaign is all-consuming."

"Tell him it's about Tom," Jack replied, watching her reaction closely. Her eyes flickered, a hint of worry, but she nodded and gestured for him to wait.

Moments later, Dan stepped out of his office, his face drawn, the warmth from the town hall replaced by an exhausted wariness. He gave Jack a look that was somewhere between a greeting and a challenge.

"Didn't expect to see you here," Dan said, folding his arms. "What's on your mind?"

Jack took a deep breath. "We need to talk. Somewhere private."

Dan hesitated, but then motioned for Jack to follow him into a back room that looked like it once served as a storage closet. The walls were lined with faded campaign posters, some dating back to Glenfield's forgotten mayors. The irony wasn't lost on Jack.

"What's this about, Jack?" Dan asked, his tone guarded.

"It's about the contracts, Dan. The ones tied to Tom" Jack's voice was steady, each word landing like a stone.

Dan stiffened. "You're going through town records now? I thought you were here as a friend."

Jack's eyes flashed. "I am here as a friend, Dan. Or I was. But this..." He held up a printout of the courthouse documents, highlighted in red. "This isn't you. At least, it wasn't the you I used to know."

Dan looked away, his face unreadable. "I'm trying to help this town, Jack. That costs money. And Tom's resources... they're what we need to make a difference."

Jack shook his head. "At what price? Tom's buying influence. He's using Glenfield like his personal bank, and you're letting him."

Dan's voice was low, almost pleading. "Glenfield is dying, Jack. You've seen it. I can't just stand by and watch that happen. If working with Tom means we get the funds to fix roads, build schools, keep businesses alive... then maybe it's worth it."

"Worth what, Dan?" Jack asked, his tone rising. "Your integrity? The trust people have in you? I know you, Dan. You didn't get into this to be someone's puppet."

Dan flinched, and for a moment, Jack saw a flicker of the man he used to know, the idealist who had once inspired him to chase the truth. But then, just as quickly, the mask returned.

"You don't get it, Jack," Dan said, his voice cold now. "You left Glenfield. You went off to chase stories and write about problems from a safe distance. You didn't have to stay here, day after day, watching things fall apart."

Jack clenched his fists, trying to keep his voice calm. "I left because I couldn't stand watching you compromise. And now I'm back, and it feels like nothing has changed."

Dan's eyes narrowed, his frustration boiling over. "Maybe that's because you've never understood what it means to really fight for something. To make the hard choices. I don't have the luxury of purity, Jack. Not if I want to make a difference."

Jack felt a chill settle over him. He had always known Dan was ambitious, but he hadn't realized just how deeply that ambition had embedded itself, twisting his ideals into something almost unrecognizable.

“Is that what this is?” Jack asked quietly. “A difference? Or a legacy?”

Dan looked away, his silence answering the question for him.

Later, as Jack walked back to his car, he felt a weight pressing down on him. This was more than a story now. It was a test of everything he believed in—about friendship, loyalty, and truth. He couldn’t let his history with Dan cloud his judgment, but he also couldn’t deny the pang of regret that gnawed at him, a lingering wish that things could have been different.

Determined, he dialled his editor at the New York Tribune, a no-nonsense woman named Sandra Jones who had a nose for scandal and an unerring sense for a good story.

“Sandra, it’s Jack,” he said, trying to keep his voice steady. “I think I’ve got something big here. A series on small-town politics, corruption, and the dark side of American ambition.”

Sandra’s voice crackled over the line. “You know I’m always interested, Jack. What’s the angle?”

Jack hesitated. “It’s personal. But I think it’s a story people need to hear.”

There was a pause before Sandra replied, her voice softer. “Just be careful, Jack. Stories like this have a way of biting back.”

He hung up, staring at the small-town skyline. He had come to Glenfield for answers, and now he was leaving with a mission. The path forward would mean risking everything, but he had no choice. This was the story he was meant to tell.

That night, Jack worked late into the evening, typing furiously in his small rented room, fuelled by coffee and a fire that wouldn't be extinguished. He traced the web of connections between Dan, Tom, and various shady business deals, gathering evidence that painted a grim picture of Glenfield's so-called "revitalization."

Finally, as dawn broke, he leaned back, exhausted but exhilarated. He had the beginning of something powerful—a story that could change everything. But as he looked at his notes, he knew that telling this story would mean shattering the last remnants of his friendship with Dan.

He closed his notebook, a pang of sadness settling over him. He was doing what he had always believed was right, but the cost was higher than he'd ever imagined.

In the dim morning light, Jack felt a strange sense of peace, as if he'd finally come to terms with the reality of his choices. He had come to Glenfield to find the truth, and he had found it—along with the price that truth demanded.

Tomorrow, he would confront Dan one last time, knowing that it would be the final chapter in their story. He was ready.

CHAPTER FIVE

The Reckoning

The town of Glenfield woke up slowly, the hazy morning sun casting a warm glow over the old brick buildings and quiet streets. Jack hadn't expected sleep to come easily, but after hours of reviewing his notes and piecing together the narrative, he finally drifted off, knowing what had to be done next. There would be no more hesitation, no more playing nice with the past. The truth was out there now, and it was his job to reveal it.

He dressed quickly and headed straight for Dan's campaign headquarters, his mind made up. He couldn't let this go any longer. Not for Dan. Not for anyone. He needed to hold the people in power accountable—starting with the man he'd once considered a brother.

As he approached the familiar old building, a knot twisted in his stomach. Despite all the years, the betrayals, the distance, he couldn't quite shake the feeling that this moment was one that would define everything. His friendship with Dan, his career, even his sense of self. There would be no turning back after this.

Jenny was the only one there when Jack arrived. She was hunched over a desk, flipping through a stack of papers, but she looked up when she saw him.

"Jack," she said, her tone neutral. "He's in a meeting. You want to wait?"

"No," Jack replied, his voice firm. "I need to speak with him. Now."

Jenny raised an eyebrow but said nothing as she gestured toward the door leading to Dan's office. Jack didn't wait for an invitation; he opened the door without hesitation and walked in.

Dan was sitting behind his desk, flipping through some papers of his own. He looked up, his face a mixture of exhaustion and something else—something Jack couldn't quite place. The air between them had shifted, and both men knew it.

"Jack," Dan said, his voice clipped. "What's going on?"

Jack didn't sit. He stood there, the weight of what he was about to say pressing down on him. "I've got everything I need, Dan. The story. The contracts. The connections between you and Tom. It's all there."

Dan's face hardened, his posture tense. He stood up, placing his hands on the desk. "You don't know what you're talking about."

"I know more than you think," Jack countered, holding up the stack of papers. "And I'm going to print it, Dan. I'm going to tell the whole town, the whole world, what you've been doing. How Tom's been using you to funnel public money into his pocket. How you've sold out everything you once believed in."

Dan's eyes flashed with anger, but there was also something deeper—fear, maybe regret. He stepped toward Jack, his voice lower but no less intense. "You don't get it, Jack. You think this is about money or power, but it's not. This town—this town is on the brink. And I'm doing what I have to do to save it."

Jack's chest tightened. "Save it? By letting men like Tom run it into the ground? You're just another cog in the machine, Dan. You're no different from anyone else."

Dan clenched his fists, his voice rising. "You think I wanted this? You think I wanted to be here, making deals with people I can't trust? You think I don't hate it? But I'm doing what I have to do because no one else will. And you—" He pointed an accusatory finger at Jack. "You left. You left when it got hard, when it wasn't glamorous anymore. You walked away from this town, from me, from everything we talked about. And now you come back, acting like you have the moral high ground."

Jack felt the sting of Dan's words, but he didn't flinch. He had been prepared for this. "I didn't walk away, Dan. I left because I couldn't watch you become this. You're losing yourself in all of this, and I'm not going to stand by and let it happen."

Dan's shoulders slumped, and for a moment, the facade cracked. There was a fleeting look of sorrow in his eyes, something raw and vulnerable. "I don't know what else to do, Jack. People are depending on me. And I can't go back now. I've already made too many compromises. I've... I've crossed lines."

Jack's heart softened, but the anger still burned deep. "Maybe it's not too late to make it right. You can still walk away from this, Dan. It's not too late to be the man I thought you were."

Dan's gaze turned cold again, the walls going up once more. He turned his back to Jack, pacing the small office as he spoke, his voice steady but tinged with something darker. "I've already made my choice. I'm not turning back now. You want to destroy everything I've worked for, go ahead. But I'm not giving up. I'm not going to let you or anyone else stand in my way."

Jack's throat tightened. "I don't want to destroy you, Dan. I want to save you. But you have to see what you've become. You've traded your soul for power. And I can't be a part of that."

There was a long silence between them. Neither man moved, neither spoke. The weight of the moment hung heavy, the air thick with years of unspoken history and unhealed wounds.

Finally, Dan turned back to face Jack, his expression unreadable. "If you're going to write it, then do it. Print your story. I'll deal with the fallout. But don't think for a second that I regret what I'm doing. Not one bit."

Jack nodded slowly, his heart heavy. "I wish I could believe you."

With one final, lingering look, Jack turned and left the office. As he walked down the hallway, he could hear Dan's voice behind him, rising again in a conversation with Jenny. But the words didn't matter anymore. The story was already in motion, and nothing could stop it.

The next few days passed in a blur for Jack. He spent his time finalizing the article, gathering the last bits of evidence, and sending it off to Sandra for approval. As he waited, the pressure of what he was about to do weighed heavily on him. He knew the consequences—how the town would react, how Dan would respond, and how it would change everything between them.

On the night before the article was set to publish, Jack drove out to the edge of town, overlooking the valley where Glenfield lay below. The city lights twinkled in the distance, a reminder of everything he was about to lose. His phone buzzed in his pocket, and he pulled it out, seeing a text from Dan:

"You won't change anything. Tomorrow, you'll see that."

Jack stared at the words for a long moment, then put his phone away. His hand gripped the steering wheel, his heart heavy with uncertainty. He had come to Glenfield to find the truth, but the truth had come at a price.

Tomorrow, the reckoning would come—for both of them.

The days following Dan's downfall passed in a blur.

CHAPTER SIX

Rebuilding the Pieces

The days following Dan's downfall passed in a blur. Glenfield was a town divided. Some rallied around Jack, grateful for the truth and eager to see change. Others mourned Dan's fall, seeing it as the end of Glenfield's last real hope for revival. As much as Jack wanted to feel relief, he found himself troubled by the ripple effects his story had created. He knew he had done the right thing, but it was a hollow victory when the town felt fractured.

It was in the quiet moments, walking down the nearly deserted Main Street, that Jack felt the full weight of his actions. The place he had grown up in was changing, its people grappling with the unsettling truths he had unearthed. He would pass familiar faces, once warm, now wary, as if he were as much a stranger to them as they were to themselves. He had expected anger from Dan, maybe even bitterness from a few who had been swept up in the campaign's promise. What he hadn't anticipated was the quiet disillusionment that blanketed the town like the first chill of autumn.

Determined to turn his investigation into a beginning rather than an ending, Jack began attending town council meetings and community gatherings. He listened as residents expressed their fears and frustrations. For once, he didn't come as a reporter but as a neighbour , a listener, someone who cared about Glenfield's future. It was humbling and, in its own way, cathartic. This time, he wasn't just exposing a story—he was helping build one.

A month after the article broke, Glenfield held a town hall. It was the first major gathering since the scandal, and the turnout was larger than expected. People crowded the old school gym, murmuring, shifting uneasily, unsure of what was next for a town that had lost its leader and its sense of direction.

Jack watched from the back as familiar faces filled the rows. Mrs. Carson from the bookstore, Mr. Leary who ran the hardware shop, Jenny, who had stepped away from Dan's campaign after the fallout, and even Tom, sitting with a smug look as if daring someone to confront him. Jack's presence was quiet, almost unassuming, but everyone knew who he was. The crowd parted slightly when he entered, some nodding in respect, others eyeing him with cautious glances.

The mayor opened the meeting, his voice shaking as he welcomed everyone. He spoke briefly about the need for new leadership and asked for input on the direction Glenfield should take. But it was Jenny, Dan's former campaign manager, who finally took the mic, her voice clear and unwavering.

"I'm not here to defend Dan," Jenny began, glancing briefly at Jack with a hint of respect. "But I am here to say that this town deserves more than empty promises. Glenfield is more than a campaign, more than any one person's ambition. We've all had a hand in this, either by believing too easily or by looking away when things went wrong."

A murmur rippled through the crowd, and Jenny continued, her voice stronger now. "We don't need a saviour. We need each other. We need people willing to put in the work—not for recognition, not for power, but because this is our home."

Her words seemed to settle over the crowd, grounding them. For the first time since the scandal, Jack saw a spark of hope flicker in the faces around him.

When the mayor opened the floor for questions, Jack stood. He hadn't planned to speak, but the moment felt too important to let pass. Clearing his throat, he faced his neighbours, feeling both the weight of their scrutiny and the tentative trust they were placing in him.

"I know that some of you blame me for what happened with Dan," he began. "And I won't pretend that exposing the truth was easy. But I believe that if we don't hold ourselves accountable, if we don't face our own flaws, we can't move forward."

He looked around, meeting the eyes of those who held his gaze. "I've been thinking a lot about why I came back. I thought I was here to tell a story, but now I see that I'm here to help build one. This town deserves leaders who are part of it, who know what it needs because they live and breathe it. And I'd like to be one of those people."

A silence fell over the room, but this time it was filled with understanding rather than tension. One by one, people began to nod, murmuring words of agreement, of encouragement. It was a small gesture, but Jack felt the shift, the first fragile threads of trust being woven back together.

In the weeks that followed, Glenfield took its first steps toward renewal. Town meetings became regular gatherings, where decisions were made collectively. Jack found himself unexpectedly involved—sometimes taking notes, sometimes offering ideas, but more often simply listening. Glenfield had found its voice, and it didn't need a single leader. It needed everyone.

Jenny, who had been so devoted to Dan's campaign, became an invaluable part of the town's efforts. She organized fundraisers, spearheaded volunteer projects, and connected local businesses with resources. Jack admired her resilience, her ability to rise above the disappointment and build something meaningful. They grew close, bound by a shared commitment to see Glenfield through its most challenging chapter.

As winter settled in, Jack took stock of all that had changed. He had come to Glenfield as a journalist, expecting to expose a story and move on. Instead, he had found himself entangled in its fabric, becoming part of its unfolding narrative. And in the process, he had found a purpose he hadn't expected.

One evening, as Jack walked down Main Street, he saw lights glowing warmly from the diner, the library, the small businesses that dotted the town. They were modest places, but together they created a quiet sense of resilience. The town was still healing, still finding its way, but it was alive, growing from its scars rather than shrinking from them.

Jenny stepped out from the community centre, bundled against the cold, and waved him over. She smiled, her eyes bright, her cheeks pink from the cold. "Walk with me?"

They strolled through the quiet streets, sharing stories of their lives, their dreams, and the road they had taken to get here. As they walked, Jack felt a sense of peace settle over him, a quiet certainty that he was exactly where he was meant to be.

Glenfield wasn't just a town on the mend; it was a place of possibility, a place where people learned from their mistakes and built something better. And Jack knew he would be there, helping to write its future, one step at a time.

As he looked up at the stars, glimmering over the town he had once thought he'd left behind, Jack smiled, feeling the last chapter of his old life close. "THE "LAST HURRAH" had become something more—a beginning, rather than an end.

Epilogue

Five years had passed since that spring, and Glenfield was almost unrecognizable from the town Jack had returned to that fateful autumn. The town square bustled with new shops, cafes, and businesses, all owned and run by locals. The once-shuttered storefronts had been revived with bright colours and fresh signs, symbols of a community that had chosen to reclaim its identity, one small step at a time.

Jack had stayed, as he'd promised himself he would. His work evolved, no longer focused on exposing corruption or chasing big city stories. Instead, he dedicated himself to documenting Glenfield's rebirth. His stories captured the everyday moments—the triumphs and the struggles—that wove the fabric of life in a small town that had learned to thrive through resilience and unity.

In those five years, Jack had become an integral part of Glenfield. He took on the role of editor-in-chief for a local paper, *The Glenfield Gazette,* which he and Jenny had revived together. Through its pages, they shared the town's stories: the opening of a new farm-to-table restaurant, the retirement of the town's beloved librarian, the start of a youth mentorship program. The Gazette had become the town's heart, a place where everyone could see their lives and their dreams reflected.

Jack and Jenny had built a life together, one that was woven from the same threads of commitment and hope that had brought Glenfield back to life. Their home on the edge of town was a gathering place for neighbours, friends, and family—a place where laughter and conversation flowed easily.

On a clear autumn afternoon, Jack stood at the edge of the town square, watching as a new plaque was unveiled outside the community centre The plaque honoured those who had contributed to Glenfield's renewal and growth, those who had chosen to stay and build a legacy that would last.

Jenny joined him, her hand slipping easily into his as they watched the small crowd gather around the plaque. Beside their names were others: Mrs. Carson from the bookstore, Mr. Leary from the hardware shop, even Dan's name. Despite the choices he had made, Dan's initial vision had helped spark Glenfield's change, and the town had chosen to remember him with grace.

As the ceremony concluded, Jack turned to Jenny, his heart full. "We did it," he said softly, almost to himself.

She smiled, a warmth in her eyes that hadn't faded in all their years together. "No," she corrected, "*we're* doing it. Glenfield isn't finished yet."

Jack nodded, feeling the truth of her words. Glenfield was a living, breathing story, one that would continue to grow long after they were gone. And as he looked around, watching neighbours laugh and share stories, children run through the square, and new families settle in with their own dreams, he felt a sense of peace that was both profound and lasting.

For Jack, Glenfield had been "**THE LAST HURRAH**", the place where he'd once come seeking closure. But in the end, it had given him a new beginning, a new purpose, and a legacy he could pass down. This town had been rebuilt, not by a single leader or vision, but by people willing to face hard truths, to work side by side, and to believe in the power of community.

As the sun set over Glenfield, casting a golden glow across the square, Jack squeezed Jenny's hand, knowing they had found something rare and precious—a place they could call home, a story worth telling, and a life worth living.

Together, they turned and walked toward their future, the promise of a new day already waiting on the horizon.

www.ingramcontent.com/pod-product-compliance
Lightning Source LLC
LaVergne TN
LVHW041302150826
845673LV00008B/2699

* 9 7 9 8 8 9 6 3 2 0 3 5 7 *